For Natalia

Back on Earth I'd like to thank:
Ma & Pa, Nattles, Nan, Jan,
Isabelle, Heidi, Heather,
Julita, Fran Brown,
some of my teachers
and all of my
friends.

All rights reserved. Published in the United
States by Random House Children's Books, a
division of Random House LLC, a Penguin Random House
Company, New York.

Random House and the colophon are registered trademarks of
Random House LLC.

Visit us on the Web! randomhouse.com/kids

Educators and librarians, for a variety of teaching tools, visit us at RHTeachersLibrarians.com

Library of Congress Cataloging-in-Publication Data
Price, Ben Joel, author, illustrator.
Earth space moon base / Ben Joel Price. — First edition.
pages cm.
Summary: An unlikely trio lands on a planet and keeps the inhabitants at bay using bananas.
ISBN 978-0-385-37311-1 (trade) — ISBN 978-0-375-97201-0 (lib. bdg.) —
ISBN 978-0-375-98194-4 (ebook)
[1. Stories in rhyme. 2. Life on other planets—Fiction. 3. Astronauts—Fiction. 4. Robots—Fiction.
5. Monkeys—Fiction.] I. Title.
PZ8.3.P916Ear 2014 [E]—dc23 2013017581

MANUFACTURED IN CHINA
10 9 8 7 6 5 4 3 2 1
First Edition

EARTH SPACE MOON BASE

Ben Joel Price

RANDOM HOUSE

Space.

Moon.

What is this secret place?

Where does it end?
Soon we'll know.

The doors slowly open.
What do you see?

A spaceman, a robot,
and a cheeky monkey!
(Have you ever seen
such a strange group
of three?)

Flying into space
on a secret task!

Taking pictures from afar,
Spaceman jets past planets and stars. . . .

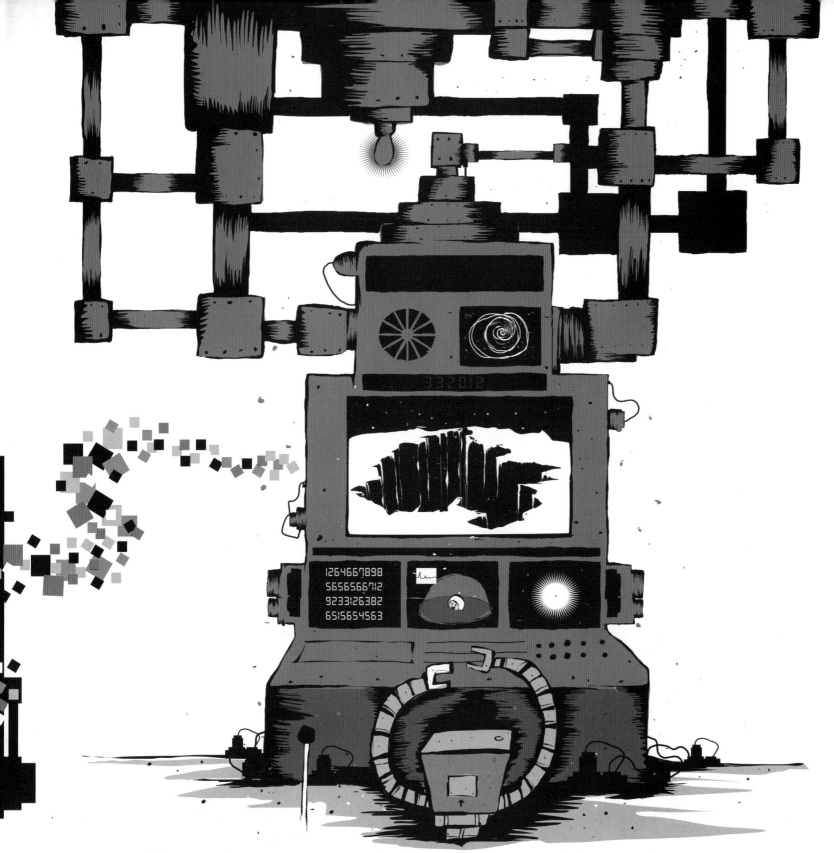

Robot's surprised at incoming data.
The monitor shows a deep, dark crater!

Monkey is sent out
to explore.

Why he's dropping bananas,
we're not quite sure.

Then, all of a sudden, something shoots out!

Tentacles squirm and thrash about!

Aliens emerge one by one,
devouring bananas
till they're gone.

SLEEPY AND FULL, THE CREATURES RETREAT.
THEY'VE ALL HAD FAR TOO MUCH TO EAT.

We're safe from the aliens,
but just in case . . .
the crew keeps watch
from the secret base.

The End?

BASE DATA
SPECIES CHECKLIST

1. SNOOLAB
2. WEEVILSHROOM
3. SQUABBLER
4. PELTWELKA
5. WINGED SPROUSER
6. BARNACLEDCHAB
7. KROBLIT
8. WUCKLE
9. SCRUNGER
10. DROMMIT
11. SCHNUFF
12. VOOG

1.

2.

6.

5.

9.

10.